The King's
Egg Dance

The King's
Egg Dance

by Larry Wilkes

Carolrhoda Books, Inc./Minneapolis

LIBRARY OF CONGRESS CATALOGING-IN-PUBLICATION DATA

Wilkes, Larry.
    The king's egg dance / by Larry Wilkes.
        p.   cm.
    Summary: A shy king, wishing to be included in the Egg Dance
celebrated by his subjects, concocts a desperate scheme involving
the disappearance of their chickens.
    ISBN 0-87614-446-6
    [1. Kings, queens, rulers, etc.–Fiction. 2. Chickens–Fiction.
3. Bashfulness–Fiction.] I. Title.
PZ7.W648388Ki   1990
[E]–dc20   90-2019
                                                              CIP
                                                               AC

Manufactured in the United States of America
1 2 3 4 5 6 7 8 9 10 99 98 97 96 95 94 93 92 91 90

For Joe and Elenor, Jan Steen,
and Prague

There once was a very shy king
who lived all alone in his palace.
He would watch the townsfolk walking
underneath his windows and dream of having
friends of his own.

"I wish they would invite me to their big
Egg Dance," he would say to himself.

The king daydreamed for hours
about joining the annual Egg Dance
—how he would dance around and in between the eggs,
trying not to step on them,
while he played the fiddle and the people cheered.

But how can it ever be? he wondered.
I'm too shy to ask for an invitation,
and nobody ever comes to the palace.
How will people ever know what my dream is?

The sad and shy king thought about this
for so long that his dinner grew cold and
the red evening sky turned to
the darkness of night.

But then the king had an idea.

That night, while the townsfolk slept peacefully,
the king made a little journey from the palace...

...and returned silently before sunrise.

The next morning was a quiet one. Oscar, the young farmer at the edge of town, was the first to wonder *why* it was *so* quiet. Why is the cock not crowing? he thought as he opened his window to let in the morning sun. Why aren't the hens pecking and scratching and clucking? Are they all still asleep? Oscar got dressed and went to look around. He made a terrible discovery.

"My chickens are gone!" he shouted.
"Mine too!" called the milkman.
"And mine!" the postman hollered.
Everybody's chickens had disappeared!

"This is terrible!" they all wailed.
"No chickens means no eggs.
And no eggs means no Egg Dance tomorrow!"

The townsfolk could think of nothing to do
but search for their chickens.
All day they looked in every corner of town,
but except for a few feathers,
there was no sign of a chicken anywhere.

Then just as everyone had given up hope...

…Oscar's rooster was seen
strutting proudly across the Square.

Then another chicken was spotted...

...jumping through a hole in the palace wall.

"They must all be in the palace!" shouted Oscar.

The townsfolk gathered together and
marched angrily up to the palace doors.
They knocked and rang the bell,
but the doors remained firmly closed.

A little nervously,
the townsfolk decided to let themselves in.

Then, as they were
slowly climbing the great stairway,
something dreadful happened.

The whole armory came crashing down...

...making the most incredible noise!

The townsfolk were unhurt, though rather shaken,
and they continued to search the palace.

Eventually they arrived
at two large doors.

Oscar slowly pushed one open,

and there,
to everyone's astonishment,
was an enormous hall
full of...

...CHICKENS!

And at the far end of the room,
hiding behind a chair, was the king!
"I thought you were an attacking army,"
said the king, trying to look dignified.

"Why have you taken our chickens?"
Oscar demanded.
"I wanted to join in the Egg Dance,"
the king said, blushing, "but I was too shy to ask."
"A little silly, don't you think?" someone whispered.

The king's cheeks turned redder.
"I suppose it is," he stammered. Then gathering
his courage he announced, "From now on,
the annual Egg Dance shall end with
a grand party at the palace—beginning tomorrow!"

Everyone cheered, and there was huge laughter
when Oscar pointed toward the floor
where the chickens had been.

There were eggs *everywhere!*

So, with no time to spare,
the festivities began.
And the king's dream came true—
fiddle and all!

About the Author and Illustrator

Over the last few years, Larry Wilkes has delighted audiences with his lively use of puppets, animation, and special effects in film, writing, and drawing. *The King's Egg Dance* is Larry Wilkes's first picture book for children. In the playful art, one can easily see how the puppets in Larry's imagination have found their way into this inventive tale.

Though Larry Wilkes was born in Yorkshire, England, he grew up in Malaysia. At 13, he began his artistic training. He later studied at the Derby College of Art in England and then finished his degree at the Sheffield School of Art. He graduated with honors.

Larry Wilkes's interest in children's literature came alive when he was raising two children of his own. Larry now lives and spins his imaginative tales in Lincolnshire, England.